UNEXPECTED

Compiled By

SNEHNAZ SHEIKH

AL – LINA PUBLICATION

Write with the passion...
We are here for your dreams...

Published by AL – LINA PUBLICATION
Chennai, India
Email : linapublication@gmail.com

First Edition : May 2022

UNEXPECTED

Presented by: AL – LINA PUBLICATION

ANTHOLOGY

Cover Design by: Team AL – LINA PUBLICATION
Book formatting: Snehnaz Sheikh

DISCLAIMER

This book is a work of fiction. Names, characters, and incidents are either the author's imagination or used in a fictitious manner. Any resemblance to actual persons, living or dead, or actual events is purely coincidental.

This book has been published with all efforts taken to make the material error-free after the consent of the writer. However, the authors and the publisher do not assume and hereby disclaim any liability to any party for any loss, damage, or disruption caused by errors or omissions, whether such errors or omissions result from negligence, accident, or any other cause.

We as AL - LINA Publication and compilers has given the effort to publish this book. If there's any plagiarized content publishers nor the compiler won't be responsible. In case of plagiarism only coauthors are responsible.

This book does not intend to disrespect any community, caste, religion, creed, nationality or gender.

This book is published by **AL - LINA Publication**

ACKNOWLEDGEMENT

This anthology would not be fulfilled without the people who owe their words for this book. I would like to thank every soul who has contributed their writings in this book as the co-author. Each of their masterpiece made this papers into the book.

I would like to thank every person who believed in us for which this anthology has become possible . It has been a wonderful cooperation with all the co-authors who have send us their masterpieces with their definition of love and affection.

Thanks and regards.

SNEHNAZ SHEIKH
Compiler

SNEHNAZ SHEIKH

Snehnaz is a student pursuing medicine and wishes to go for a journey to spread elixir of emotions through words as a vagabond.

Tales under the lanes

Life can be monotonous at times
wondering how time flee away
smouldering our journey of hope
while drooping with responsibilities.
Plugged earphones with music on
and the daily commotion passing by
not knowing how each story peddles through
unescorted by the meddling of chores.
Uncertainty of each emotion
traversing a thousand faces ,
demanding new journey,
craving for adventures
to venture out the sophomore .
Tranquility of the life has gone way back
dreams realising us ;we are alive .
Beguiled by the images of future
racing with oneself
leaving the past by winds
caressing the face with tiny drops .
Perplexion heading over
and the ticking time binding around
recreating each day .
Heavenly hours of lying over
while we procrastinate
having the passion buzzing
in a mood of snooze .

CO-AUTHOR DESK

1. Fadiya Folakemi Omowumi
2. Debahuti Borah
3. Dr. Sadiya Sulatana
4. Vaneeta Chugh
5. Amninder Singh Mangat
6. Raima Sen Sharma
7. Shweta Shekade
8. Acharya Ashish Pandey
9. Amisha Gupta
10. Sachitha
11. Ratan Nath
12. Hemalata Madiraju
13. Jawahar B Lalla
14. Jamali Layne
15. Payal Surani
16. Kshitij
17. B. Raji
18. Shivalika Singh
19. Tehreem Khursheed
20. Kulsum Yasmin
21. Rangeesh Chandrasekar
22. Shahnaz Akhtar
23. Aakriti Midha
24. Rutvik Patel
25. Akanksha
26. Shanaya Rajput
27. Vaibhavee Soni
28. Hansika Bhagwani
29. Muralidhar Bansal
30. Mrs. Sarita Srivastava
31. Nidhyapriya C
32. Amlly
33. Payal Agarwal
34. Johann Zara

FADIYA FOLAKEMI OMOWUMI

Oluwafolakemi is a young girl. She's a Nigerian and enjoys expressing her thoughts and emotions through writing and hoping that one day she'll be good enough considering she knows she's not the best there is.

It's over

It is over!!! That was exactly what I said to love...until you To say it only started with a glimpse of you sitting in the congregation that day. I can remember vividly how your eyes were monitoring each of my every move. I knew you were watching so I tried my best not to look at your side. After the service, though at first it was awkward, but I was excited to stand close to you You came to greet me and I am sure I felt butterflies dancing in my belly. Tho you disappointed me by not asking for my contact. I tried to hide my disappointment but deep down I was pained. Leaving the church premises I couldn't get the thoughts of you out of my head. My head felt so cloudy I couldn't think stray, probably why every guy I saw reminded me of you. Fate worked it's charms and we started talking. It was if I've known you all my life. You're all I dream of and And all I want. You compliment me so well, it felt too good to be true Even when I said I won't fall in love again, I fell helplessly and nothing could hold me With each day passing, my love for you grew Even the tick tack of the clock only reminds me of how perfect my life has been since you entered It is amazing cos I know you feel the same way about me. I can't explain to myself how it happened. Tho it was unexpected, yet it is the best thing that ever happened to me.

April's fool

Everything was going on well that morning until we heard the knock on the door. My sister ran to open the door, we all looked at the door waiting for whatever awaits us there. It was Joy, my dad's secretary. She entered and sat down looking down. We were all excited to here what she has to say. She just shrugged off and told my sister she was bored at home and came to our place to feel better. We all laughed. She does that a lot, trying to make us think something was up until boom she breaks the tension with her indifferent story. That's so Joy. Suddenly we heard the loud and angry voices from my parents room. That is so unexpected. Tho daddy and mummy fights once a while but they never yell. We hardly even know when something is up. What shocked us was that daddy practically packed his bags out and kept on shouting that he's leaving us for good. The biggest shock landed on us when he pushed Mummy and looked up to Joy and said "baby let's go" Even my mummy that was holding her back looked up immediately, Joy?? Baby?? We were all shocked as dad and Joy left us with our jaw hanging. So it was her all along, she comes to our house to eat whatever food my mummy prepares, wear my mom's accessories and even sleep in our house sometimes. So she it was her. We couldn't even stand up or move from our position... Then daddy and Joy ran inside to scream April Fool!! Yeah it was 1st of April.. I can remember how we spent the whole morning begging mom.

DEBAHUTI BORAH

Debahuti Borah is a poet and writer from Jorhat, Assam. She did her BA in English (honours) from St. Anthony's College, Shillong; and proceeded for MA English (honours) from University of Hyderabad. She loves to read, write, travel, and listen to music. She is also passionate about modelling, being a freelance model for many years. Her inspiration for poetry and short stories comes from the rawness of everything in this universe. She wants to reach out to others and believes in the power of hope and kindness. You can reach her at debahutiwrites@gmail.com

Roses I wore a black plain T-Shirt which was wearing off. I was wearing off inside with no pillow to scream into. I was walking home from work, completely dazed. I had not slept in two days. I was exhausted. Fatigued. Vehicles passed by me, honking loud, as I came to a standstill. I looked at this tiny stall by the footpath in the busy, traffic-affectionate juncture of Bangalore city. I couldn't help but look. I looked at the pretty, fresh flowers neatly stacked on the left side of the stall. There were roses, chrysanthemums, lilies, and some more which I was too tired to recollect the names of. On the wooden stool sat a mother - draped in a green saree - as if she was the tree that nurtured these flowers. And she did nurture them with fresh water, to nurture herself and her little daughter who sat on her lap. Their eyes yellow, their lips dry. I realized they had not been eating, drinking, resting properly. The crowd around me was hurrying past me and I just stood there, shaken. I slowly moved towards them. The mother's eyes shone up with eagerness. I knew right there that I needed to do something. I had a five hundred rupee currency note with me. And I asked her for two roses for five hundred. She looked at me, stunned, and said in Hindi, "Madam, it's fourty rupees for two roses." I smiled at her, pushed the five hundred rupee note into her shaking right hand and briskly walked away with the two white roses I had selected. I stopped abruptly. I turned. I walked back to the mother and daughter. The mother was looking back at me, shocked and teary-eyed, while the little one wailed - probably out of hunger. I went to her and smiled, with my eyes tearing up a little too. The mother said, "Madam, I don't have change for five hundred-" I cut her short, "Don't worry. I am here to gift you and the little one some flowers," while I gave the roses to both of them. The little one stopped crying and looked at the rose in her hand, and the mother stood there, fumbling a "Thank you" that came right from her soul. I said, "Eat well and go get some rest." That day, after reaching home, I slept like a baby - happy that I can help someone in whatever capacity I can. The Goddess of Sleep didn't punish me that night.

DR SADIYA SULTANA

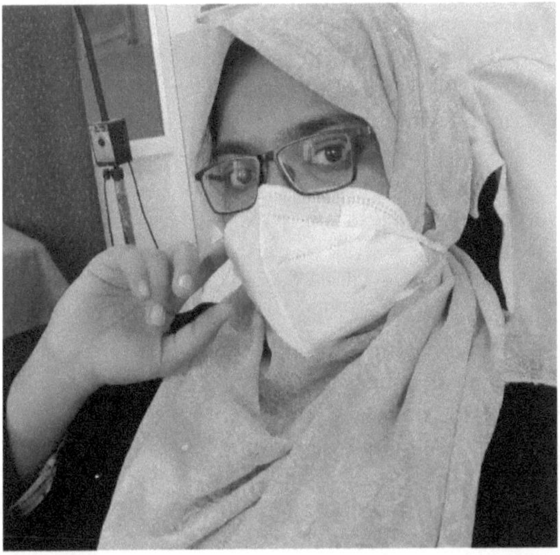

This is Dr Sadiya Sultana, a practising doctor from Hyderabad. Writing serves as a medium to express freely all that she could never dare to speak. The power of ink inspires her to write more, aiming to spread positivity around and to heal people through palliative words.

LIFE - A BLESSING

Learn to value every moment of your life
Because you never know which is actually the last
There are people who fought to survive
in their last minutes, but they had to depart

You think your problems are the biggest
Know that you're blessed in many ways
You can breathe the air, walk on earth's crust
and prevent yourself from the sun's rays

You're given good health, you mobilise
and adapt all the ways that keep you strong
The price of health, only they realise
who have faced the illness for too long.

MASKED IDENTITY

Everyone these days behave so odd
You never know their identities are masked
Their pretence seems too real to you
Causing you to trust them so undue
Later when they exhibit the real self
You then think who's wrong - you or them
And till you realise their deception
They already blame you for every action
And you begin to convince everyone
With proofs against their accusation
Yet your statements they constantly reject
Your evidences they begin to suspect
And that's when you feel too dejected
With your Lord you stay connected
Because He's the only One who knows your innocence
And He could surely restore your acceptance

VANEETA CHUGH

Vaneeta Chugh, a graduate in b.com and diploma in special education V.I, a resident of delhi. She has been looking through different perspective towards the world since she learnt the meaning of life and somehow writing became that source for her. She started it out as desperation and salvation; but, eventually, it became her life. She has been a part of more than 5 anthologies till now and would be of many more to come.

Once a song

Once a song that broke my heart
Once a song that broke my heart,
My ghost unsung its lyrics in the cementery,
Necrolived corpse of a beautifully broken bride, inlaid,
Your name engraved upon the carousel of my bleeding soul,
Besides the grave of your lost armour,
I had never cried before that hypothalamus day,
but the, Dam flooded in incessant volley of lamentation,
The moment I heard you were engaged,
And that to the only "soul-sister" of mine,
The one with whom I had shared all my secrets and lies,
The fallout was an egregious aide-memoire,
Your chest pieces hellishly scorched in ashes, albeit,
Mine plagued with searing erotic pretence of yours,
case of Homicide indeed!
I was erring with possessiveness of love..

Unforseen

Be like the drizzling diamond droplets, who are meteoric for the most part, unforseen with the speed of lightening, bringing love and woye at your doorsteps with no prejudices and boundaries! Not the rainbow, which is predicted as well as foreseen, conditional within limited timeline.

Embrace the unexpected! Because life is never predictable, lest you would be struck in a rookie jar of ifs and buts. Challenges bring out the rainbow flavours upon your frozen ice cream, bittersweet to taste, yet soulful to the heart afterwards. Memories are the marbles decor on your wall of mind, once colourless and soulless, should be ebbed off and pristine saffron moulded with rose couloirs must be piled on the wall unhackneyed, glistening in the shade of new beginnings.

AMNINDER SINGH MANGAT

I'm a 26 year old boy, it would be hard to tell how I came to write, it was just a feeling that took me with me, the worldview is a little bit different, so I enjoy reading books, and traveling. I am also fond of traveling, I am always honest with myself, I have never intentionally harmed anyone physically, financially or mentally.

Path

This life is a path and we are all walking on it,
it is not necessary to meet the destination
but it is necessary to keep walking
because it is not necessary
to meet the destination in such a birth,
so the first duty of all is to take
their own path If the time is right,
the destination will be found by itself.

Misunderstanding

Sometimes just
Misunderstandings occur,
With the son's father
With mother's daughter
With friend's friend
With lover's lover
Or someone's with someone
Behind the breakdown of every relationship,
Let's talk

RAIMA SEN SHARMA

Hey Guys ! This is me , Raima Sen Sharma, a 19 yr old free , optimistic and a fun loving young spirit. I have passed my first year in BSc. Microbiology Honours from Scottish Church College, Kolkata and currently pursuing my first year of undergraduate studies in Medicine because serving humanity is my true and ultimate passion . Hope you would like my write up and appreciate as your appreciation would gonna further encourage me to write more pieces further in near future ! Happy Reading ❣

Expecting the Unexpected

Hey this is me Josephine, I am cute chubby girl of a mere 16 years of age but I don't look look like one ! I am a quiet,shy girl and sitted at one corner of the class. I am extremely introvert person hence don't interact with others much .But yes I am extremely good at academics and is always in good books of my teachers especially of my class teacher, Mrs. Roza Gomes who happens to be the teacher of my favourite subject, Science.Talking about my family, I have a sister Nancy of 2 years old , my caring daddy and my loving mom ,so a close knitted family of four. But things took a different path when my mom died at a tender age of 35 after 5 years long battle with leukaemia. Soon there was a nanny appointed for me and my sister as father was most of the times away from home due to official tours.Coming to present, I was walking down alone on the little pavement by the main road , introspecting about my weakness,career and future. I had put on my headphones to a bit old school sad music and suddenly I change my mind to cross the street to visit the nearby park across the lane . And guess what, the bad day struck , I failed to notice the truck coming at a high speed from the opposite side,and I was too late to move away and as far as I remember the next moment I could see everything dark and passed out .The next morning, I woke up and discovered myself in the hospital bed with a slight uneasiness in my left leg. I heard doctor uncle telling to my father that I won't able to walk again ! I was so sad and depressed, disheartened but I didn't cried before them and acted as I have heard nothing.

Father bought me home after a week . He was unaware that I already overheard the doctor's talk . But as days passed by, I slowly woke up from the bed and keep moving on the wheel chair. Nobody cared and supported me as much I needed. I could feel that Papa have distanced himself from me. The nanny used to be busy with Nancy most of the times.

After a year , I was confident enough, I started going out all alone of the house with the help of my wheelchair. I never tried to walk because whenever I tried to take the initiative, the doctor's hopeless words haunted me. So one fine day , I was passing through the same unlucky pavement , lost in my thoughts as usual . Suddenly my eyes caught hold of a small kitten crossing the road and a car in a high speed coming from the opposite side. I involuntarily cried out , " Oh

Jesus ! Save it !" , I gathered enough courage and confidence to leave the wheelchair independently and managed to run with my right leg and as much as strength my left leg can give me , swooped down at the kitten , cuddling it managed to save it by a narrow escape. Unexpected incident right ? I gonna refer it as miraculous. A huge crowd gathered around me , gave a lot of appreciation,applause, blessings for my courage and strong spirit. Later on the highest official of the city police department gave me an award of bravery and appreciation.

That unexpected incident gave me enough strength and motivation to walk by myself and sometimes I could walk without my wheelchair in the home doing my daily chores. My daddy heard the entire incident from our nanny once he was back from his official tour and finally broke down . He asked me for forgiveness and promised never to distance himself from us again so I at once forgave him because I loved him a lot. So once again we were back like a close knitted family like the earlier times. Though sometimes I still miss my Mommy , but I still remember that "unexpected " miraculous incident vividly which helped me to win back my dad's hope, family's love and my optimism which enabled me to dare to dream !

Adieu !

SHWETA SHEKADE

Shweta Shekade resides in Mumbai. Her work has appeared or is forthcoming in numerous places. This is her fourth anthology. She is a National volleyball sports player. And also a good writer

Unexpected

When unexpected moments happen in life, they bring us varied emotions.

Unexpected things in life may bring us happiness, excitement, fear, enjoyment, surprise, and much more. This is why, in life we should always embrace (and sometimes do the unexpected. The best way to deal with life is to acknowledge and accept that unexpected things can happen in life. Once you accept that surprises are a part of life, it will become easier for you to deal with them. As you do not have any control over the unexpected things, it is always better to prepare yourself to adapt to any life situation.

Whenever something happens that u never expected, you enjoy that with more happiness. When u meet someone unexpectedly and they become the most important part of your life, you never thought that you could find someone who could be this good friend of yours, you find good friends, you spend enjoyable unexpected moments with them which eventually make u happy.So, enjoy these moments as unexpected moments, surprises as they give u happiness more than anything

ACHARYA ASHISH PANDEY

Ashish Pandey, He is a resident of a village named Parasara in Sultanpur district of Uttar Pradesh. Along with studying Sanskrit, he has a special interest in Sanskrit literature and Hindi literature in his life, .He has resolved to increase Hindi and Sanskrit literature till the end of his life. With his special experiences at his young age, he is continuously setting a new example for literature. He has made many contributions in the work of writing and devotion and will continue to do so, he is a lecturer of Bhagwat Katha and studying and teaching in the college. He has written and continues to write many books. They want to do some special research in their life, they want to give a new history to India, on which they are constantly thinking.

Unexpected

Childlessness when the moment comes Such incidents happen in life what man does not know, and happens, suddenly there is a change in life, and everything is scattered like wind,Just as a garden is destroyed when a storm comes,Human's unexpected moments hurt a lot,Suddenly coming like a time or say like deathSometimes life gets better and sometimes it doesn't Suddenly everything falls apart and suddenly everything is foundHow can I describe the unexpected moment, it is the wind, it just comes.

Unexpected moments come like the wind, Who shakes a man and gets nothing Just like a lion caught in a net cannot do anything.

Amisha Gupta

Amisha Gupta, is in college and is doing B.A. in English Literature. She lives in Raipur,Chhattisgarh, India. She lives with her family who has supported her in each and every step. Reading and baking is what she loves the most but writing is what comes out unexpectedly. Reading has inspired her the most in her writings. Besides studies, she loves reading in her leisure time. She will practice to write the best and hard to put down stories for her readers in the upcoming future.

WE MET

"…And when she realised that she was suffocating, the diary on the table whispered something to her and that's how she was reborn."
Kai closed the book triumphantly which he was reading on a train journey. A girl across him casually asked Kai,
"A book lover? Can I get a review of it?"
"Nah! A bibliophile. The review.."
He remained silent for a minute and stared at the book on his hand.
" Well this book is phenomenal. The rainbow of happiness, the rapid heat of hardwork, the rains of sadness and the stormy clouds of darkest days. But it hasn't failed to include the sunrise of hope and a new beginning. My first read of Alora Jones, wanna read more. I wish I get to meet her soon or probably an autograph from her."
" I guess I should read it then."
" You should. Mind guarding my things? Be back soon."
" Sure."
When Kai got back the pages of the book was fluttering by the wind. As he was about to close it, his gaze fell on the first page.
" Hi! Bibliophile." And the signature of Alora jones was there. But the girl was gone.

SACHITHA

She's a young writer from the queen of hills who's persuing her bachelor's degree in chemistry.A poet, keyboardist, lyricist, artist.She aspires to do everything that makes her happy.

Awful moment

In my headphones
Only his songs I used to hear
In various zones
I had no fear
Looks so handsome
Sings beautifully
Waited for him to come
I stood very shyfully
One day , in my mobile
I received a random text
I danced from a mile
I replied him with emojis next
Unexpectedly happened to me
I was so much happy
A big fan always to be
Favorite soul making me wrappy.

RATAN NATH

Ratan Nath is a student pursuing masters in political science and has a interest in writing and acting. He has been a part of the journey to write his emotions through words and wishes to continue learning with the experiences in life . Writing is one of the best way to express your emotions when he can't say anything he writes and believes it be a great example of healing with connections.

Anxiety and depression.

Hey stranger, I know how much pain is hidden in your brain and you can't express how much you suffer in alone. I know how it's felt when the enemy is in your brain a day started with anxious mind end up with panic attacks, I know how it's felt living with constant anxiety and depression. I know how it's felt when you passed night without sleep, I know you have suicidal thoughts in your mind and sometimes you think to commit suicide but you don't, but even the worst day of your life, when You feel like, You don't have hope for living don't worry this is not the end, the way will find you by his own way, and the universe will save you from this, everything will be normal again believe in this. Healing comes from accepting it and take medicine do meditation, try to socialize do what you love to do and hope one day it will disappear you'll be normal like others and it'll be part of life and stay with you forever but a little part. What you have to do is hope from worst days to hope for better days.

Scared

I am scared of people,
Not from love.
I am scared of being cheated or broke,
Not from staying forever.
I am scared of losing faith from love,
Not from losing the person i trusted most.
I am scared of staying with fake people
Not from staying alone.
I scared of sad ending,
Not from happy ending.

HEMALATA MADIRAJU

She had done her masters in Business Administration. She knows four languages i.e. English, Hindi, Telugu, Marathi. Apart from being a home-maker and a mother, she writes short write-ups likes poems and quotes. She is an avid reader and occasionally reads non-fiction and web-comics. She is an astrophile, a hodophile and photography lover. She is languages enthusiast , currently learning Korean. Also, she is an indian and kpop music fanatic.

Unexpected Heartbreak

Future seems to be pleasant,
With someone unknown,
Felt like match made in heaven,
Present full of smiles and roses
With no thorn exposures,
Full of understanding for one another,
Was their belief about each other,
expectations from and for each other,
Little did she realise life was not the same later hereafter,
Shattered and broken for her love was just a token,
For his wishes to be a fulfillment,
Life turned the way round,
Unpredictable leaving her lonely heartbroken.

Your voice and speech is your biggest asset when it improves the quality of relationships in your life and increases the value of people around you.

Hesitation in expression will never let you know what you are like and what you are capable of.

Words of hurt or humiliation are like pest that infect the green fields of the mind. A daily dose of meditation and self-consciousness prevents the hurt from entering our minds.

JAWAHAR B LALLA

He is Jawahar Lalla. An accomplished senior management executive, writer, blogger, speaker, panel judge, book reviewer having more than 36 + years of rich and vast IT technology experience. My articles on the Industry domain has also been published in Indian and Foreign publications I have been invited by many conferences & seminars organizers to be on their judge panel & speaker. I have also been involved as a book reviewer for many technology & management groups. Co-Author in more than 70 Plus anthologies books. Winner of numerous awards, E certificates in writing.

Email: jawahar_72002@yahoo.co.in.
Instagram Ig: JBLwrites

Hello Friends

Every day I come across good souls & bad souls.

Good souls give me positive vibes & talk positive things while bad souls only give me negative thoughts & are full of jealously keep arguing & fighting.

Why most people aren't appreciative of someone's success & popularity????.
Human beings are a social soul who wants to share those key achievement feelings with people with who they are connected & are in their network.
The feeling of those moments is so ecstatic when we want to share something with someone or on social media, we eagerly await people responding.
We all live & want to celebrate those special moments with each other.
We should be appreciated and be part of our family friends', relatives' success this is what life is all about??.
We need to be appreciative & not criticized in our life.
Isn't it wonderful & leaving our good thoughts in other peoples minds?

JAMALI LAYNE

My name is Jamali Layne but I write poems under the alias of Almost Reverie. I chose this name as reverie means a daytime dream. The reason I added almost to it is because my days consists of dreamlike occurrences but always fall short of such as a result of some tragedy.

Unexpected

Unexpected is a weird word to use,
As I always knew I wasn't the one you'd chose.
To my surprise you'd look my way,
But never having enough time to spend the day.
Oh is it a crime to like somebody older?
The more she keeps herself guarded the more I want to hold her.
I did not expect a day would come like this,
You let your guard down and we finally kissed.
Such a feeling I will always remember,
Funny how bringing it up always strikes your temper.
Yes you do like someone much younger than you,
But to say you feel the same way as I wouldn't be true.

PAYAL SURANI

She is Payal Surani living in Vishakhapatnam. She had completed a diploma in computer sciences. Recently, she realized that she can pen down her thoughts too. So she just started engraving her emotions on a paper and instantly fell in love with writing. She feels that loving is easy but expressing the same thoughts multiple times is tough and unconditional. She can write poetry and short stories in Hindi and English as well.

Until we meet again..!!

He tried very hard to open his eyes but failed miserably. The continuous ringing of his mobile wanted him to throw it to the wall. After a few seconds, the ringing went off. He did not bother to look at the caller as his head was swirling like a wheel. "All thanks to the quantity of liquor I had last night," he murmured, taking his head in his hands. He got out of his bed reluctantly as his system needed his coffee, a strong one indeed. He headed to the kitchen and just as he started moving his hands, his phone rang again. He slowly went and looked at the unknown number for a while before picking it up. Before he could even speak a word, the girl on the other side started yelling like there's no tomorrow.

"Where the hell were you? I tried calling you for like a million times now. Okay, don't answer that. Listen now, so it's like he wants to meet in a cosy cafe and not in any restaurant. So now I am thinking about how to dress. Should I pick some casual denim or should I go with a sundress? Maybe I'll go with..,"

"Oh miss. Whatever your name is, please give me a moment to speak and give yourself a moment to breathe." He spoke sarcastically as he was not in one of his best moods.
She paused for a while and spoke after realising her blunder, "Oh, sorry. Wrong number." She hung the phone without even giving him a moment to speak.

"What a good start to the day!" He said to himself in mockery while rubbing his drunk head irritatingly.
He stopped the car with a jerk pressing the brakes forcefully. As soon as he enters his favourite coffee shop, his throbbing head starts soothing. "This was the peace I was searching for." He whispered while taking his usual place. It was his go-to place whenever he wanted to relax or to concentrate.
He needed not to define what he wanted to have. His hazelnut latte was served with chocolate almond cookies as usual. As he took the first sip of his latte, he experienced his hangover flowing out of the window.

"Pure bliss," he whispered.

Just as he was munching on his cookies, he heard a deadly familiar voice. His eyes inspected the whole place and stopped at the owner of that voice. She got big eyes with enthusiasm clear in them. Her hair seemed soft and was flowing in all directions because of the mild wind and she was trying to manage them with her hand while sipping on something that looked like dark chocolate.
She seemed like a perfect blend of innocence, mischief and maturity. She got a smile that would light up the whole gloomy place effortlessly.

"Would you like to repeat the order, sir?" The server asked, breaking his chain of thoughts.

He thought for a while and nodded in answer. He again thought about where he heard her voice as he did not remember seeing her before. Then his eyes went wide with realisation. He heard her the same morning on the phone. She was that unknown caller. He never failed to recognise voices once heard. He wanted to go and talk to her but something inside of him did not permit his legs to move. He just sat there looking at her talking and moving so casually yet beautifully.

He was not the kind of a man who would stare at someone like that. But as we say, we all break our self made rules for someone. And it seemed like she was that someone. He started staring at her like he could break all the walls made by himself around his heart just for her.

She stood up and was ready to leave. He became restless as he could not speak to her. He stood up abruptly taking his book in his hands and was ready to talk to her but she was nowhere to be seen. After paying his bill he turned and got hit by someone. It was the same girl who came back to take the book she forgot before leaving the place. Both the books fell and both of them locked eyes for a few seconds. "Hey, sorry did not notice that you were just behind me," he spoke softly.

"It's perfectly fine, as I was in a hurry too," she said, giving him her bright smile. After a good pause, he decided to break the silence, "Good that you chose that cute sundress over denim. The black colour suits you well." Her expressions yelled that she was in pure shock. She did not understand what he said for a while. Just then they both looked at the titles of the same book they carried, lying on the floor.

"Until we meet again..!!"

Sometimes, some stories don't need a complete closure. Leaving some of them incomplete, seems beautiful.
Coincidences and surprise meetups speak more reality. Some unplanned eye locks are more than enough for losing yourself in them.

Just meeting someone for the first time or for the last time depends totally on destiny. We cannot get control over some scenarios that occur without our consent. Even if we run from ourselves, fate has its own verdicts.

Kshitij

Kshitij is a young talented and experienced writer with writing experience of more than 4 years with more than 70 poems in different languages Nepali, Hindi and english.

Welcome to the world of oceans

Oh dear, Welcome to the world of oceans
Carrying the waves of currents in motions
These waves looks beautiful indeed
Jump into the depth of it
And yourself find the truth of dead

The death of humanity
The death of love
The death of beauty
The death of soul

I jumped into the deap ocean
Found my deities buried inside
I took shivling in my hand
And asked " Why are you sitting in ocean instead of mount kailash"

He dropped a tear and said
"What's the point of worship when they pour all the milk to the drain instead of giving to poor"
I took laxmi in my hand
And asked " Why are you buried here
Instead of sitting with your narayana"
She smiled and said
"What's the point of being worshipped,
when they use me most in a wrong way,
Call bribed money as laxmi"
I took saraswati I'm my hand
And asked " Why are you also buried inside
When you give knowledge and wisdom.. They need you "
She pulled a string of sitar and said
"What's the point being, when they take wrong things instead of knowledge and wisdom"
I took Lord ganesha in my hand
" Is there any solution, oh superior "
He smiled and said
" What's the point of worshipping us when there's no humanity
First go and purify your heart with love and affection "
Oh deities, thankyou for showing me the path
I will go out to the cruel world

and give this message by the Lord.
I jumped out of the ocean of truth
And said the world
Oh people, why do you worship
Oh dear, why don't you first go and purify your heart.
There's no point of worshipping God
When your heart is full of darkness
"Every heart is where God lives"
You always say this
But you yourself say
"Don't touch the idol, you are untouchable"
You yourself say his impure heart will touch devine purity.
No one is born dalit
No one is born brahmin
Please stop being judgemental
Hear this beautiful calming
unknown sound of silent waves
And make yourself worthy
To worship your deity.

B.RAJI

B.Raji is from madurai. At present she is pursuing her first year of M.A in English literature. She loves writing her memoir. Furthermore with her ingenuity in the version. She has been a co-author.

Let it happen

Instead of expecting us to be what we are,
Let it happen. Happiness is what we
Get when we are unexpected with surprise. Our minds yearns to think of it
When it does not happen to us in
Anticipation. But how much joy the mind
Gets when our favorite things happen
When we least expect it.

Try as much as we can without looking
Forward to anything and find
Success in it.

SHIVALIKA SINGH

Shivalika Singh writes as a positive outlet for her emotions, it helps her to make sense of her pain, as you say, at least use your pain for good writing material. She hopes and wishes that her words help someone to feel they're not alone in this miserable and terrible world, that they have someone who has felt what they feel. She hopes to connect with her readers soul, to make them feel a little bit less alone, to offer them even momentary peace, that is what she considers her success.

Love tries

Love tries to remain kind,
It is the departure that seems cruel,
Every word remaining yet all meaning in them lost,
All the love stays but the one who is loved, is lost,
Every memory of joy turns sour,
You don't know where to put it all down,
This broken shattered heart of yours,
Coz you cannot let it go,
Coz you haven't learnt how to,
You pull it like dead weight,
Like a ghost chasing you day and night,
Wherever I go, is still here.

The illusion of choice,
The feeling of control,
Is the best recipe for disaster,
For losing that which you held,
Is far worse than losing
that which you had never gotten hold of,
The taste of blood only turns bitter,
The warm sun eventually burns off its recipient of light,
The water which ends up shattering the mould with too much movement.

TEHREEM KHURSHEED

She is an observer, an introvert, and a writing enthusiast who writes, rants and reads whenever she wants. She firmly believes that everything can be fine with a cup of coffee. A lover of stars, moons, skies, forests, oceans and everything of nature. She carries a certain wilderness and abyss inside her.

Sudden

All it takes is a sudden phone call,
A sudden sight, a sudden turn on the road,
A sudden flash of light, the sudden realisation
Or a sudden mishap,
To alter the direction of your life.
The way life brings surprises to us;
indicates how vulnerable we are,
And how we are nothing but the audience of our lives.
Under this open sky,
We are spectating the greatest unfolds of realities,
The way every moment reveal itself to us,
It makes us drowned in amazement.
In this collapsing world,
The only thing that you can expect is unexpectedness.

Is it a glass
Or is it my memories of us,
which is gently shattering?
My vision is getting fogged now,
I am forgetting your face, your fragrance now.

You were expected to return healthy,
You were expected to breathe fine,
But the unexpected path you took 7 years back,
Make my heart ache to this day.
I am now scared of fading memories of ours.
So I am waiting for the day, the moment,
When we will meet on the other side of the world.

Kulsum Yasmin

Kulsum Yasmin from is an Indian poet living abroad completing her medical studies. who loves books, coffee and clouds over people. She completed her studies abroad and is pursuing a medical career. She hopes her writing would relate to people on the other edge and would soothe people who are in pain and distress.

Oh dear

Oh dear ! Worry about yourself
After am gonna change
When you feel things get strange
You set the fire on stage
Just make the move to evolve
And give yourself the chance
To grow out from your own rage
To the looks you exchange
Burning them in their own cage
They will move to make their chase
After when I made them erase
And from the mistakes I embrace .
You never know
I stay there online for you
Looking at you
So as to when things creeps me
It feel you beside me
I stay there online for you
When anxiety troubles me
I say you are with me
Even distances apart
You stay in my heart.

SHAHNAZ AKHTAR

She wants to make the world a better place with limited resources at her end. She strives towards understanding humans and their emotions, but can't process emotions too well, ironically! She wants to break from the monotony and bondage of society, bit by bit.

Unexpected Endings

Things change;
Time passes by,
People let go of emotions too easily,
Find a new attraction and get attached;
Those old feelings are suddenly detached;
In darkness and silence I sit,
Where do these broken pieces exactly fit?

Those ideals and promises are gone,
Just like an old forgotten song;
The heart fails to acknowledge what the mind knows,
But, with time, the realisation sinks in;
The blurry vision is now crystal clear,
The weak heart is now devoid of fear.

Shattered dreams but memories intact,
Memories with which I wanted to break contact,
Noticing a smile build up about my lips,
I gather the strength to look at my trembling fingertips;
You are stronger than your fears, I say;
Life taught me a lesson to be remembered everyday.

RANGEESH CHANDRASEKAR

Rangeesh Chandrasekar is a MBA Finance and Marketing graduate staying at Chennai. He is passionate about writing and a great lover of books and articles who has Co authored in 800+ anthologies.

My Dream Proposal

Everyone had a dream in their lives. But my dream is differ from others. My dreams all about, my dream proposal. My thoughts are all about my future!

If someone needs me in their lives or if someone needs my company to accompany their rest of their lives! I dreamed lot of times, based on my unfilled desires. But this moment completely differs I can't able to guess, if it is real or reel. That moment my eyes are filled with glorious pleasure. My lips are murmured been like - "Wake up boy, it's all your dream!"

But my soul told, make your heart too bold. Unexpected proposal make me bliss. My cheeks are turn like a rose petals. My dream life entered in my real life. Unexpected moment happened to wake me up, so finally I heard my soul voice with heart melting words!

Be my life until my life comes to an end. God create someone to cared me a lot. Thank god at finally I found my Ms.right in my hazy life.

You are my light to make my life bright!

Unexpected Fate

I was spending my life with your memories and then suddenly one day my biggest fear came true, which I dreaded the most! I had a report in my hand which had my fate written in, and I still was not ready to accept the reality! The fate which God had written for me was brain cancer! The day when I saw you laying in the white box with your eyes closed, I felt my heartbeat stop! That day I promised myself that I will make our love last lifelong by remembering you through the memories we created together over the years! But I did not know that God will steal my one and only happiness away from me! I am sorry that I could not keep up my promise dear, but I hope in my next life I will get to live a longer life with you!

AAKRITI MIDHA

Aakriti Midha loves writing and has a habit of writing whenever she wants to express herself, through her writings. Her poetry are related to her or she gets the inspiration of choosing the theme of the poem from the stories. She loves listening to people and helping people through their hard times. A graduate from Delhi University she started her own small business during covid and kept writing poems and short stories. She loves animals and is a lover of nature. She loves it when people relate and love what she writes. She wishes that you will love these too. Happy Reading!.

The Unexpected Happiness

I was at my lowest
Seeking comfort in my loneliness
Toxic relations and friendships
Killing me and all my feelings

Unrevealed memories and the torture
These were just some of the guilty pleasures
The heart was just tired
Fighting the self-harm thoughts
And ashes of half-burned cigarettes in the corner

Unexpectedly, I found THE one
Who actually understood my pain and sorrow!
The one who stayed by my side
Through the good and the bad kinds.
I was blessed with happiness in the most unexpected of times.

They taught the meaning of self-love
And pampered me enough
They made me realize
The world is not cruel
Only some people are!

Self-harming thoughts disappeared
My heart found comfort
In some people that were strangers
And now the reason I find myself enough.

The Moments Worth It

There are some moments in life
That tends to change the way you are
The suffering and pain
Starting a fire of burning hatred
That eats you alive

You end up hating everyone
Even your own life that seems cruel
Unexpectedly some people enter
Who makes it all better and fine

Some people who care more than you dreamt of
Who loves you enough that you forget the hate
The one who proves that love is mightier
Than the sword that you picked

The one person that changes
The way you looked at the world
They change your thoughts and ideas
By just being who they are

How simple this life is
And how much we can complicate things
It's in our nature to hate those
Who we don't seem to vibe with

I saw all the moments
The bad and the good
And it changed me into someone
I hated too

Some unexpected care and love
From the people close to my heart
Made me learn to love myself again.

RUTVIK

Rutvik Patel Is an Engineer And Love to write

Loved by you

I allowed myself to be loved by you.
Moving from across the street to a building that I always wondered what was inside.
I am not at all innocent.
Allowing myself to become busy.
Never really having the time to indulge in something I always wanted to do.
A new building in a familiar place.
So welcoming.
Freeing myself of everything around.
The clock loosely ticking away.
The world no longer the same.
The steps taken from across the street becoming my favorite.
Remembering the first time I looked at you.
The term busy no longer existed.
Allowing myself to come at ease.
Opening the door.
Crazy how everything just happened.
Doing something unexpected, forgetting that I had something to do.
I allowed myself to be unexpectedly loved by you.
Completely forgetting where the door was.
Losing track of time.

Sometimes i feel so distant
i even feel like crying
without knowing why
& it makes me feel lost.
i don't want to go back
to the depressing days
when i could hear voices in my head
& had insomnia
neither to have depressed & suicidal thoughts.
i thought i got over it
i thought i overcome it
but no;
i didn't really do.
you can't just overcome something
that has being with you for years.
maybe you feel better & better
as the time passes,
but depression will still be there
deep inside you
waiting for you to have a moment of sadness
so it can seize you again
& you better be prepared for it
because it can get you
without you expecting it -unexpectedly.

AKANKSHA

Akanksha is a writer and also an author . She was born on 02 - october-2003. She is from Bilhaur Kanpur. Her Father name is Mr. Rajesh Kumar and Mother is Mrs. Geeta. She also created a blog which is generally based on personal uses and daily motivation and it's name is Selfhelpblog. Generally She loves to write quotes for her blog and also provides basic knowledge to people about the business and daily hacks and many more information .Her quotes are already published in the book name of "Patriotism :Devotion to Country" in hindi recently and also published some poems and articles in different books and sites.

Spare some time

Spare some time for yourself too,
Lest one day you forget to meet yourself....
We don't blame the circumstances,
the blame is on the creator of the circumstances
we will definitely improve them one day ,
the wait is only for the right time and opportunity.....
We don't have the habit of pretending in front of people ,
Yes we just want to do as much in which we can be happy.....

You are in me and I am in you,
What a strange relationship is that
You are in me and
I am with you .....

Of course ! There is a lot of difference between you and me but life is the same inside both.....

Don't talk about the soul,
It is with you ,yes of course!
The body is with me here,
But the life is with you .....

SHANAYA RAJPUT

Mellow writings matched with a vivacious personality, Shanaya Rajput, currently a student, is an author in the making. The writings in her journal often center dark themes of nature and human emotions. Being a highly imaginative person, her hobbies include daydreaming and scribbling flowy pieces. She has a love for all things sweet, abstract and deep.

Treachery

What was supposed to be medicine,
Transformed into disease itself.
Like a stain, ever growing
Like a vial of poison, ever brimming.
It was bound to happen.
Just like waves bound to crash
Or the night bound to fall.
No more hidden, it was out in the open-
Like a secret on a serpent's tongue,
Like a full moon, deep set in velvet black.
Yet somehow, to these bones,
This warm blood and sword of a gaze,
It came stealthily, unknowingly-
Like a stab in the back.
It came when it was expected least.

VAIBHAVEE SONI

The poet, Vaibhavee Soni is an avid writer. Based in Bangalore. She has an Instagram page dedicated to her writings with the username - @__strawberry.lemonade__ . As her Instagram username suggests her poetry has a bitter-sweet essence to it just like strawberry lemonade. She has had a knack for weaving poetry since a very young age. Her muse can either be her real life experiences or her vivid imagination. She loves being creative, unique and different in her writing, she aims to create an identity for herself through her words. The greatest validation for her is when a complete stranger resonates with her work. She takes personalized orders for writeups or poetry , if interested please contact her through her Instagram. Apart from writing she loves to indulge in any creative activity be it fashion , acting , dance or theater. Art is her way of liberation and she believes writing is her greatest escapade from the mundane reality.

I smile wistfully

I smile wistfully as I write this...
"***I wish there was a way to know you were in the good old days before you've actually left them.***"
The unprecedented pandemic stole our desired perfect ending.
Our life , it's incredible occurring moments , special milestones , sweet fruits of our sheer hard work ....all remain unfulfilled.
Our entire sense of normality was wiped away cavalierly by a virus.
We couldn't even bid adieu or say a grateful goodbye to our past , it just vanished so suddenly, it breaks my heart.
It's like pages of the awaited climax got ripped off from the book of our life.
The race stopping before the finish line.
The rollercoaster slowing when we want it to speed.
None of us got a definite conclusion , our ending remains elusive.
Unending questions scrambling our mind , answers unsaid..... We wait in vain for '***The End***' :
-of our unfinished wishes , hopes and dreams that were planned.

Reminiscing wavy memories 🌊💔

Candy cane mist swayed in the sweet sea breeze,
Silken sea grenades bursted in my beach brain.
Iridescent glow on the sequined shore,
Mermaid scales bounced through feisty foaming whisked waves.
Turquoise turtles befriended coffee salted sand,
Braided bread lay on crisp checkered table cloth.
Castle clouds roamed slowly,
On the royal ramp of the shimmering skyline.
These mesmerizing maeve mornings,
Adorned the collection of my pastel past.
The prudent pandemic stole my soul's solace ,
Left me with empty eyes and a yearning for my beloved beach that I can't replace.

HANSIKA BHAGWANI

Born in city of Nawab- Lucknow, India. She is sweet, simple and helpful in nature therefore she feeds and take care of stray babies most of the time. She is Hansika Bhagwani, a beginner currently studying in Class 12. She discovered her writing talent when she wrote her first poetry and then started gaining her interest in writing. She received immense appreciation on her first poetry. As people were able to connect their emotions with her. They think she writes very simple yet it is very deep. And she is here to connect you all with her emotions and feelings.

I'M IN LOVE AGAIN..

I think I'm in love again..!
But, this time everything feels so different.
Different from my past love.
I don't know what it is.
How to even explain this?
Those stupid butterflies again and the heart that beats so fast.
Crave of having his touch, looking into his eyes, the warmth of his hug, and him by my side always.
The sense of his smell is still in my mind, causing me to think about him more often.
But, this time night is beautiful, not sleepless
This time it is happiness, not sadness
Or a feeling of being alone in the darkness.
The feelings are different now the person is different,
So am I.
And,I want to feel love again, and I guess he too.
I guess we are ready for love again
I guess we are ready to fall for each other.

MURALIDHAR BANSAL

He is muralidhar bansal from nepal he loves writing and started writing when he was a student. Playing cricket and writing are his hobbies.

Unexpected

It is said no one moves for long in life. But unexpected moments do walk for long and help in regaining moments.

Unexpected moments are hidden. But its visibility can be felt in the loneliness.

Unexpected moments can't be felt by those who erase it, but it can be felt by those who live in it's moments.

No matter to what extent we try to forget the bygone days, but these are still hovering around us; perhaps to gather some new way of living.

Unexpected moments can't be forgotten by forgetting. These come and go like the shadow in the brightness.

Not all moments gain momentum. Some are forgettable, some are kept for great moments while some of these remain in heart for eternal.

Unexpected moment is that seed of a plant which when watered with courage of moving ahead can bring the fruitful moments in future.

Unexpected moments are also strange at times, we often memorize those moments in life which are rather rude and nightmares.

MRS. SARITA SRIVASTAVA

Mrs. Sarita Srivastava belong to the land of Unnao, Uttar Pradesh. She has served as Principal in ICDS training Centre. She has an educational qualification in M. A (English & History) , M. Ed along with Business Management. She is keenly interested in trying recipes and has been continuously motivating students to move up in life & achieve their goals Achievements :- 1) first prize in story by kala splash 2) Newly Published Book - KNS treaty of survival .

Life

The life is full of moments that are unexpected,
Some leave such an impact that the future gets affected.
The Dream of being with the lovely souls,
Sometimes reduces us to their wandering roles
Such was one when my parents left accidentally for better world,
Leaving the 14 year old me to the mercy of others.
I, then tighter my belts and rose my sword in the mighter times
To snatch from the destiny what ever belonged to mine.
But the whole journey gave me a lesson to learn,
We should be self dependent to stand and earn.

NIDHYAPRIYA C

Nidhyapriya C is an amazing silent soul and thoughtful mind. She completed her graduation with education and Pursuing her Master degree in Coimbatore. Whatever happens she loves and putting into her writings. Never tired of writing and achieving.Criticism is also a parts of life which moves us to go forward.she loves to cook and interested in Calligraphy.

Hopeful love

In my Butterfly days, I saw
A honey bee which was hot and sweet
It well playing football gamer
Quickly I grab his arms around
Never knew what going to happen
Could be heard throughout the room.
Something special has planned before
A short trip to entertain you
What will it be?
I am wondering so excitedly
Time seems to go so slow
Hearing another car driver by
Could be the real faith with
The hopeful love with mercy!!

Amlly

He is a writer.

So much

There is too much in my heart
Some of me some of your part
There is so much in my mind
Something is bad something is kind
Something is love something its opposite
I dont know how to fix it
How can i can these circumstances
How can i make you mine.

Something i want to speak
Thats hurting my heart constantly
That damaging my smile regularly
Words are more than i love you
Words are more than i want you
But these are not enough world in this fucking world.

PAYAL AGARWAL

A pen player of feelings love to express the heart with the words of the world wish to give an ease when someone is seeking a way to reduce the pain

Her Sacrifice

Mishti and Kuhu, are two best friends but more than like sisters. They both live like, both are related to blood but some relations don't need blood to be real.

Mishti and Kuhu eat together, live together, and wear the same color clothes they both opt for the same subject, biology.

They both used to go to the same college where kuhu starts liking a boy, Adhyansh Singh, who is a whole girl's heartthrob. He has perfect charms and a Greek god-like body with sharp features that can make any girl fall, but one thing is very good, he's his Mumma's boy, who is always after to fulfill his Mumma's every wish.

College fest was going on where he first time met Mishti and Kuhu whose attention was only hinged on food. Both were holding plates with lots of varieties.

On one hand, all the students were enjoying the fest but here both the girls were busy with their food as people called them 'foodies'.

" Mishti, listen, my plate has not enough space left. Where should I adjust this dish?" Kuhu asked Mishti, who was also facing trouble, to adjust their food plate.

" Adjust anyhow," Mishti answers Kuhu without looking at her.

(Laugh****Laugh***Laugh)

Suddenly they both heard laughing voices and found four boys who were laughing at them.

First, they both check their face and clothes and then look at those boys who were still laughing at them.

Kuhu marches in their direction with the full range of anger in her eyes and stops in front of them.

Kuhu folds her hands and asks arrogantly, " Why are you laughing? Do we both look like clowns?"

" Oops, sorry, actually we were just...." Mihir Rawat, Adhyansh's friend was about to answer when Adhyansh pinched him a little to shut his mouth.

" No actually, you both are so cute that my idiot friend is finding a way to talk with you two beauties, right Mihir?" Adhyansh asks him, giving a glare. "

" Yes, yes, he is right. Can we become friends?" Mihir extended his hand to shake with kuhu but instead of shaking their hand, kuhu turned his hand around and said in his ears, " I know you guys very well what you were up to do. Okay. So don't try to be smart"

Mishti came ahead and tried to stop kuhu somehow but kuhu wasn't

ready and said, " No Mishti, you are too naive. You don't know how to handle these assholes".
Hearing the kuhu's answer, everyone turned their head to see the sight and found an angry kuhu.
Adhyansh smirks and whispers to Mihir's ear, " Dude, you may lose your life . It will be good for you to ask for her forgiveness otherwise, this wild girl can do anything worse".
On Adhyansh's suggestion, Mihir asked Kuhu's forgiveness and ran from there.

****

Days pass like this, after the incident, Kuhu, Mishti, and Adhyansh become good friends and start helping each other in their studies. Soon their final exams start. Mishti was preparing for her exam but Kuhu was lost in her Lala land.
Mishti notices this and shakes Kuhu to bring her back from Lala land and remind her to prepare for the exam.
Exam Day***
Mishti and Kuhu reached their classroom and found their different seating arrangement.
" Oh no, that's bad. We both have different seating arrangements. Now, how I'll ask you during the exam. Shit yaar. " Kuhu said while making a palm on the bench.
" Aww, you are too unlucky. Mine is too good because Adhyansh is sitting with me. I can ask him any question. He will tell me happily." Mishti mocked the kuhu and made a pout.
Their final exam of the year came. Adhyansh was sitting with his group when Mihir asked, " Dude, when are you going to propose to our dear bhabhi (sister-in-law)."
" After our last exam, I'll propose to Mishti, but make sure that the lizard Kuhu isn't present there, otherwise she'll destroy our moment". Adhyansh said lizard to Kuhu and Mihir choked.
Their last exam finally ended, Mishti and Kuhu were sitting in the cafeteria when Adhyansh entered there with a bunch of roses but to his bad, Mishti got up and left the place without noticing Adhyansh. Kuhu also follows her. She also didn't notice him which made Adhyansh hurt.

***

It was raining continuously, Mishti and Kuhu both were dancing and playing with raindrops when an SUV came and stopped in front of Mishti's house.
A lady steps out with a young decent boy and enters the Bhanushali

Mansion.
Looking at him and that too with his mother, Mishti and Kuhu both were stunned and their heartbeat started beating fastly.
Both Mishti and Kuhu shared their looks and ran inside where Mishti's parents were greeting Meenakshi Singh, Adhyansh's mother.
Geeta Bhanushali, Mishti's mother gave Mishti a cold look which was enough for her to understand what she was telling her.
Mishti enters her bedroom and quickly changes her wet clothes into one.
Mishti entered the hall with kuhu and greeted Meenakshi but to Mishti's surprise Meenakshi made Mishti sit between her and Adhyansh and said, " You are too beautiful with each other ."
Mishti smiled a little but her heart was pounding so fast that she started playing with her scarf.
" I think we should give both of them a little space to talk" What does Mrs. Bhanushali say?" Meenakshi asks with a broad course
" Of course, Kuhu child, go and take both of them to Mish, I's bedroom," Geeta told Kuhu and only nodded her head.

***

Both were sitting but Adhyansh was only admiring Mishti's beauty and said without any delay, " I can't wait to get married".
Mishti smiled at his words and said, " have some patience".
He scratched his back head and then came out after chit-chat.
Kuhu was fuming in anger and left Mishti's house without informing her.
Dheeraj Bhanushali and Geeta Bhanushali, Mishti's father and mother, fix their marriage after fifteen days.
In fifteen days, Mishti and Adhyansh both came very close to each other but Kuhu started ignoring her.
After the two days of the wedding, Mishti sends Kuhu her wedding invitation card but Kuhu makes an excuse to not attend Mishti and Adhyansh's wedding.
Mishti feels bad about loop behavior and starts finding the reason.

***

Mishti was sitting in her bedroom in a bridal dress and was looking very happy but soon her smile went away when met Karan, Kuhu's brother who starts cursing Mishti for Kuhu's sadness and tells her that Kuhu loves Adhyansh. Mishti shattered badly and left her bedroom.

***

Srishty, Mishti's younger sister came down to inform something important and quickly brought her parents and Adhyansh with his

mother to Mishti's bedroom where her bridal attire was all scattered with all the jewelry.
A handwritten letter was placed nearby the table, in which write that, " I'm sorry Adhyansh, Mummy, Daddy, Meenakshi Aunty, but I can't marry Adhyansh because I got a call letter from London with a very big opportunity chosen I've chosen my career. I can marry after some time later but I won't get this opportunity ahead. "
That was written on the note. Adhyansh fell to his knees and shattered badly whereas Kuhus was also shocked to find Mishti's selfishness.
In the age of anger, Adhyansh held kuhu's hand and took her to holy fire, and decided to marry her.
They both finally got married. Adhyansh And Adhyansh's family accept Kuhu wholeheartedly but Adhyansh was still losing Mishti's thoughts.
Mishti was looking at everything behind the pillar and was getting happy to see her best friend and her love get married happily.
A lone tear escaped from her eye to sacrifice her love but was happy that she had sacrificed for her friend who is more like a sister.
Mishti left Delhi without informing anyone but she took lots of memories of her best friend and her love Adhyansh.

" SACRIFICE IS GREATER THAN LOVE, CHARACTER IS GREATER THAN BEAUTY, HUMANITY IS GREATER THAN WEALTH, BUT NOTHING IS GREATER THAN FRIENDSHIP".

Mishti's sacrifice proves her true love and strong friendship, both".

JOHANN ZARA

Johann Zara was born as a Malayali girl who dreamt to enter the world of fantasy. Growing up, she was fascinated with reading, and this interest steered her being drawn to stories related to the romance genre. But at the age of 28 her being bedridden for a few months impelled her to explore online platforms and nurture a passion for writing. Moreover, she likes to unwrap and scatter her thoughts to achieve her dream to be an incredible author. Hence, her fantasy realm flourished through her first book Zara's Destiny.

A Bundle of surprise

Chapter 1:

I accelerated my car as I got a call from my friend. He just informed me to meet him at Blue Mount hospital and he says it's urgent. I can sense his urgency and the place of meeting triggered my anxiousness. I soon reached the hospital premises. Eric approached me as soon as my car halted in front of the patio of the hospital. He recklessly pulled me out and yanked my car key. He then heaved it to the security. He is sweating badly and anxiety is adding a paleness to his face. I have never seen him in this state before. I am surprised. "Eric… please hold on… say to me what's the matter…" I stopped him. But he is not in the sense of hearing a single word. He dragged me. Soon we reached the OT area. He then took some papers from the nurse station and gave me a pen. "David… sign here.." He ordered me. I am alarmed. What do I need to sign? I blink twice. "David… Do you trust me?" Eric's eyes showered with anxiety noticing my hesitation. "Of course… I trust you…" I don't need to think twice about that. I trust him more than myself. He was my friend who was with me when I was going through bad phases in my life. "Then sign it" he pointed to a slot. Soon I signed the paper which he showed me. Why should I doubt him? Noticing my act, the emotions in his eyes grew wider. His face gleamed brightly. Why? Before I can ask him. He took the papers and rushed to the OT. He knocked on the door. Soon a nurse opened it. "Didn't her husband reach yet..?" I saw a nurse enquiring irritatedly. "He reached… and those are the papers you want… just hurry up…" Eric said hurriedly and nudged those papers into her hands. The nurse surveyed the papers where I signed and stared at me. I am shocked to see her furious eyes. "Don't you have any sense… how can you be so ignorant when your wife is in a critical condition…" the nurse yelled at me and shut the door at full force. I stood there with wide eyes. Even my eyeballs were out. I can feel it. I am surprised… shocked… amused… Wife??? How come I have a wife? I am not married yet. Then who is that?

Chapter 2:

It took a long time for me to come back to reality. I subconsciously turned back to see whether the lady's husband was standing behind my back. Sometimes the nurse might have said to him. It's just misconceived by me. But to my disappointment, I didn't see anyone. But the nurse was peering at my signature on the paper and said those words. I then gazed at Eric. Sensing my confused eyes on him he soon lowered his eyes. I can see a sense of guilt in their face. Did I do something wrong by believing him? My heart began to beat fast. I took slow steps toward him. I don't want to acknowledge what I heard. So I need to talk to him and clear those words. But before I could enquire, the door of the OT opened again. I saw the same nurse. She came near me and carefully handed over a bundle that was draped in a cloth. Subconsciously my hands hold it. I stared at the nurse without knowing what it was for. "Hold it tightly… He was so delicate so don't loosen up your hold…" the nurse said tenderly looking at the bundle in my hand. "And… Congratulations" she said with a smile and immediately fled from the scene. My hold tightened as she said to tighten it up. But wait… why did she say, "he" for this bundle? And why did she say congratulations? I slightly gazed at the bundle. But soon I opened my eyes widely to see whether I was hallucinating or not. I can see a tiny face popping out of the draped cloth. It's a cute baby and he is smiling. A smile shaped on my lips but soon it vanished remembering her whole conversation with me. Wife? Critical condition? He? Congratulations? "David… I'm sorry…" a voice pulled me back from my thoughts. I gazed at my best friend with a confused look. But what he said gave me another shock. "He is your son…" he said with a smile. I stare at him for a while then at the baby. If he is my baby I would be the happiest person in this world. But how can he be my son? I don't have a wife. Then suddenly I got a son. It's something fishy… "David… Actually…" Before he could clear my confusion, the OT room again opened and gave me another outstanding shock. I saw a lady lying on the bed closing her eyes and a nurse dragging it out. Closely watching the face of the lady I was shocked. Soon the past phases of my life came in front of me and my eyes filled with tears. Ellena… My love…

www.ingramcontent.com/pod-product-compliance
Lightning Source LLC
Chambersburg PA
CBHW050022170726
48282CB00025B/507
* 9 7 8 9 3 9 4 7 0 2 1 4 1 *